A IS FOR AHOY

A Young Sailor's ABC

by Mitzi Ware

Illustration by Eleanore Edson

© Text copyright Mitzi Ware, 2013
© Illustrations copyright Eleanore Edson, 2013

Published by Ahoy! Press
Charlottesville, Virginia, USA

Designed by Josef Beery.

For
James Beale Cooley

If you're game to go sailing, and are just a small person,

Take a look at this book for sailing rehearsin'.

It's for young sailors like you,

So you'll know these terms through and through.

1

A is for AHOY.
It's how we say hi!

**B is for BOAT.
Climb aboard. It's dry.**

B is also for BOW.
It's located up front.
The back of the boat's the stern,
But we'll get there in turn.

C is for CLEAT.
It holds the lines tight,
C is for COMPASS.
That helps us steer at night.

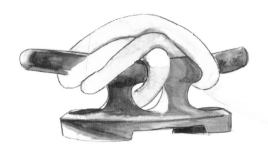

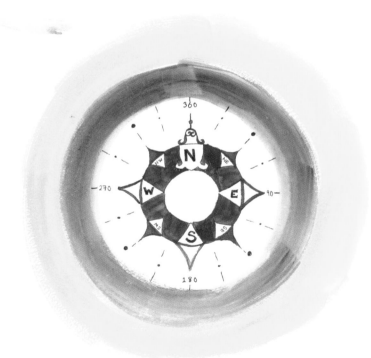

D is for DINGHY.
The boat open and small
We use it to row out
To the sailboat, so tall.

E is for EAST.
A direction to go.
It's the opposite of West,
Which you do need to know.

F is for FOG.
That thick, soupy weather,
When it's around it's not safe
To go sailing together.

G is for GAFF.
The spar at the top of the sail.
We say "spar" to mean
pieces of wood,
Confusing, but don't you turn tail.

H is for HALYARD.
The line that pulls up the sail.

I is for INLET.
A place we can hail!

J is for JIB.
The small sail in the bow
Don't you go forgetting what bow
is somehow!

K is for Keel.
The upside down triangle
under the boat,
Made of wood or of metal,
It keeps us afloat.

L is for LUFF.
When the sail flaps and shakes,
We always want the wind in our sails,
So we do what it takes.

M is for MAST.
The spar that holds up the sail.
It's tall and strong,
To withstand any gale.

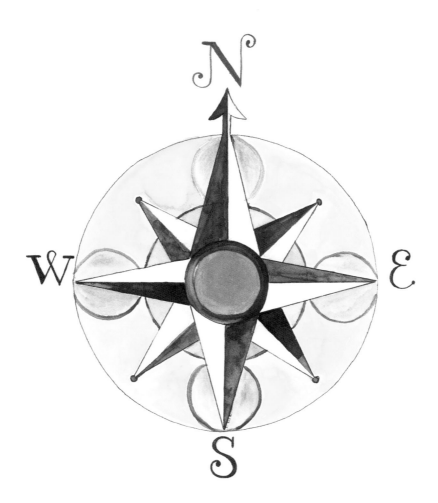

N is for NORTH,
Another direction to go.
It's the opposite of South,
For the compass says so.

O is for OARS.
We use them to row.
When the wind drops to nothing,
And we don't have a tow.

P is for PORT.
All things on the left of you,
As you look towards the bow,
On the ocean so blue.

Q is for QUIET.
No motor sounds here,
Just the sound of the boat
Cutting through water so clear.

R is for RUDDER.
The piece in the water
Right off the stern
It helps you to steer,
Which makes the boat turn.

S is for SAIL,
The cloth attached to the mast.
When it catches the wind
We go forward quite fast.

S is for STARBOARD.
The right side looking toward the bow.
Remember port is left.
You'll learn these words somehow.

T is for TILLER.
The spar we hold to steer.
It's attached to the rudder.
Are things becoming more clear?

U is for UNDERWAY.
Moving forward on the water,
We're off on our way,
If the crew does what they ought'r.

V is for life-VEST.
What you're already wearing.
It keeps you safe,
When you're out there sea-faring.

W is for WIND.
It fills our sails and we go.

X is for the eXCELLENT
and eXciting
Times we'll have sailing,
we know.

Y is for YAWL.
A very large sailboat, which
someday you may sail.

And Z-Z-Z's are for the
sweet dreams,
You'll have of your
adventurous tale.

31949974R00033

Made in the USA
Lexington, KY
01 May 2014